Abra Kadabra

**Other books in the
Shooting Star series:**

Abra Kadabra

MAUREEN BAYLESS

Cover by
RON LIGHTBURN

Inside illustrations by
JALEEN MARLES

Scholastic Canada Ltd.

Canadian Cataloguing in Publication Data

Bayless, Maureen, 1959-
    Abra Kadabra

ISBN 0-590-74759-2

I. Lightburn, Ron. II. Title.

PS8553.A95A2 1993   jC813'.54   C93-093666-3
PZ7.B3A6 1993

654321   Printed in Canada   34567/9

*For all kids whose parents
are a little bit weird.
And for my brother, Tom.
(Remember that time . . . ?)*

Contents

Chapter 1

An Old Problem

Abra had a problem. Two problems, really. Two 165-year-old problems. Her parents.

Mr. and Mrs. Kadabra had never been ordinary. At least, not in Abra's lifetime. But she'd never really thought of them as problems before.

Not until her teacher, Miss Karp, decided that the whole class would put on an Olden Days Fair. And that all the parents would come. Had to come, in fact.

"Just think of it," said Miss Karp, waving her

skinny arms in the air. "We'll all be dressed as pioneers. We'll build a fort in the schoolyard. And we'll bake bannock and . . . and . . . What else did pioneers eat?"

"Pemmican!" shouted Reuben. The class had been studying pioneers, and so practically everybody put up a hand. Everybody except Abra.

"Maple sugar!" called Kyra.

"Rabbits!" yelled Smog. And everyone went, "Ooh, yuck!" because the class had two pet rabbits.

Abra didn't say anything. She knew very well what pioneers ate, because she ate exactly the same things. Every day.

Abra's parents were pioneers. Real pioneers. In fact, they still lived in the 1800s.

Mr. and Mrs. Kadabra were ghosts.

And it is very hard to bring ghosts to school, even if they are your parents. They hadn't been to a single parent-teacher meeting yet. Miss Karp was getting suspicious.

"So," said Miss Karp, looking hard at Abra, "I

will get to meet your parents. At last."

"They might be out of t— "

"Out of town?" guessed Miss Karp.

"Out of time," mumbled Abra. But Miss Karp didn't hear.

"Nonsense!" said the teacher. "The fair is more than two months away. I'm sure your parents will be able to plan their busy schedules around that. Even if they are . . . ?"

"Historians," said Abra. "And they kind of take their history seriously."

Miss Karp wrinkled her forehead and said something that sounded like, "Poor dear."

The teacher wrinkled her forehead a lot when she talked about Abra's parents. Abra figured it was only a matter of time before she called the social workers. The only thing that had kept her from calling them up to now was that Abra always got good marks. And Miss Karp believed that good marks were a sign of a happy home life.

That's why Abra absolutely had to get an A in history. Even if she knew for a fact that almost everything Miss Karp said about pioneer days was wrong. Even if it meant building a fort in the schoolyard.

But what if the only way to get an A was to bring her parents to the fair?

Chapter 2

A Perfectly Good Name for a Ghost

"You know, Ma, you really should have named me something normal. Like Jane or Haley," said Abra, passing Ma a shovel.

"Abra is a lovely name, pet," said Ma. She took the broken handle off the shovel and put a new one on. Ma and Pa were gold miners.

"You know what I mean," Abra said. "*Abrakadabra*. Why didn't you just call me Open Sesame?"

Ma smiled. "It is a bit of a pun, isn't it? But we

are ghosts, your father and I. We were expecting to have a little ghost baby. And Abrakadabra is a perfectly good name for a ghost."

"Yeah, right," sniffed Abra. She'd been through all this before with her mother. How surprised everyone had been when Ma and Pa had had a baby that wasn't a ghost. But then, Ma and Pa had been surprised to have a baby at all. Ghosts don't, as a rule.

Abra sat down at the washtub and began scrubbing. She was the only kid in school who had to wash clothes by hand. She was pretty sure she was the only kid who did homework by candlelight. Who did not have a fridge. And whose parents rode mules to work.

"Ma." Abra cleared her throat.

"Mm-hmm?"

"Miss Karp wants you to come to school."

Ma scraped the dried mud off the shovel with a stick. "Well, bring me my quill, pet. I'll write another note."

"No, Ma, you don't understand. You *have* to go to school. We're having an Olden Days Fair.

6

And the parents have to help."

Ma went out the back door and hung the shovel on a rack. Abra followed her.

"You know that's impossible, Abra. If I go out the front door, I'll be in the twentieth century. And in the twentieth century, no one can see me."

Abra's house was the oldest house in Granite Falls. So old, in fact, that someone from the city had come out one day and nailed a sign to the door. The sign said,

Egerton and Clementine Kadabra House.
Built 1862.
Part of Granite Falls' rich heritage.

Even the city didn't know how much a part of Granite Falls' rich heritage Abra's house was. Because inside the house, it was still 1862. And if you went through the back door, the Cariboo Gold Rush was still on.

Ma and Pa looked real enough inside the house. But the moment they walked through

the front door, they became invisible. Except to Abra, who was sort of a time traveller.

"Ma, don't you think it would be easier if I changed schools? I could go to school in 1862 instead."

"That's my time you're talking about, and Granite Falls doesn't have a school in my time," said Ma. "How's the laundry coming?"

Abra ignored the question. "Well," she muttered, "I'm really stuck! No school in your day, and no parents in mine!" She went back to scrubbing petticoats.

"And that's another thing," she went on. "Nobody washes by hand any more. They buy washing machines. And they buy other things, too. Like computers. Hardly anybody writes their reports out by hand these days."

Ma clucked her tongue. "And I have such a good recipe for ink, too. What a shame."

"Greetings, kin!" said Pa, stomping the dust off his boots and coming in the doorway. Pa always said that. He never said "howdy," like in the movies.

"Sorry I'm late, Ma," he said, giving his wife a peck on the cheek. "The mule needed a new shoe."

"Pa," said Abra, "you have to go to school." And she told him all about the Olden Days Fair.

"Well," said Pa, tugging on his scruffy beard, "I'm right honoured. But I'm afraid Miss Karp is out of luck. Found a lot of gold in my pan today. I'm pretty sure I've struck it rich this time. Have to keep at it, before someone else gets it."

Abra sighed. The trouble with her parents was that they just didn't understand how hard it was to be a kid these days. They didn't take anything seriously. Not even Miss Karp.

"Look," Abra said. "Our whole class is going to dress up as pioneers — "

"No problem, pet," said Ma. "I'll lend you my overalls."

"And we're going to make pioneer food," continued Abra.

"Pioneer food? Is pioneer food different from other food?" Pa scratched his head.

"Miss Karp is going to boil maple syrup for candy," Abra told him.

"Maple syrup! In Granite Falls?" Pa guffawed. "There's no maple syrup in Granite Falls, not in my day. She must be thinking of some different pioneers."

"Well, she just moved here," said Abra patiently. "But she's got this book. It's called *Pioneers in Upper Canada* — "

"Well, that explains it, pet," said Ma, emptying Pa's gold dust onto the scales. "Those Upper Canada pioneers are softies. Couldn't look a grizzly in the eye if it ate their supper. Only the finest pioneers come to the Cariboo."

"Came, Ma. Came to the Cariboo. The gold rush has been over for a century," mumbled Abra.

"What?" asked Ma.

"Nothing. Only, it doesn't matter what Granite Falls is like in your day. I don't get marked on knowing that. It's what's in Miss Karp's book that counts."

"What did you bring for supper, Pa?" asked Ma.

Pa held up a wiggling gunny sack. "Tender young rattlers," he said.

Abra shook her head. And they wondered why she never brought anyone home for dinner!

Chapter 3

A Town Full of Bad Guys

"Achoo!" Abra sneezed.

"Oh, dear," murmured Ma. She felt Abra's forehead. "You have a fever. I'd better fetch Doc."

"Aw-w, Ma!" grumbled Abra. "Doc'll just want to use leeches." Doc always used leeches, no matter what was wrong with her. To suck out the bad blood, he said. If she broke a leg, he'd probably use leeches for that, too.

"I'll just get an aspirin at school," she said.

And sneezed.

Outside, she met up with Reuben.

"Why don't you just use Kleenex?" he asked, looking at her hanky. The one Ma had cut from an old shirt.

"It's a long story," answered Abra.

"What kind of pioneer are you going to be?" Reuben asked.

Today was the day they had to tell Miss Karp what they were going to be for the fair.

Abra shrugged. "A gold miner, I guess."

Reuben snorted. "You can't be a gold miner! Only men were miners."

Abra stopped walking. She pointed to a statue of one of the town's founders that stood in front of the school.

"What do you think Goldpan Annie was? A dentist?" Abra retorted. "You don't know anything."

"Yeah, well, I know just as much as you."

Abra didn't say anything. How could she? Goldpan Annie was her nanny, but Reuben would think she was nuts if she told him that.

"Well, I'm going to be a sheriff," declared Reuben. "I already have a sheriff's badge." He showed her the badge on his sweater.

"A sheriff!" Abra hooted. "This isn't the wild west."

Reuben looked at her in surprise. "Of course it isn't," he said. "But it was. That's why the fair will be so much fun. I'm going to be Sheriff Cooper, and Smog is going to be an outlaw."

"Okay," said Abra, rolling her eyes. "You're right. You're ab-so-lute-ly right." Let Miss Karp tell him that sheriffs were only in the States. Granite Falls had Royal Engineers. And Judge Pointer.

In class, Miss Karp had a hard time getting everyone to stop talking. Finally, she clapped the chalkboard erasers together. Hard. Chalk dust flew everywhere.

"Now, class," she said, twirling. (Before Miss Karp had moved to Granite Falls from California, she had been a ballet dancer.) "One at a time, tell me what characters you've decided to be."

"I'm going to own a saloon," said Mark. "The kind with swinging doors. Saloons are good places for shootouts."

Miss Karp nodded and wrote it down.

"I'm going to be a bad guy," said Smog. Which was just the right thing for the class troublemaker to be.

"Me too," said half the class.

"And I'm going to be the sheriff and drum up a posse," shouted Reuben. "Who wants to be my deputy?"

Abra waited for Miss Karp to straighten him out, but all Miss Karp said was, "Wonderful idea, Reuben." Then she wrote down Kyra's name as deputy.

By the end of class, there were nine bad guys, a saloon owner, a sheriff, a deputy, a jailer, four cowboys and a corpse. And one gold miner. That was Abra.

"You call this a gold rush?" Abra grumbled, then sneezed. "Cowboys? Outlaws? Who's digging for gold?"

"A little under the weather today, are you,

dear?" clucked Miss Karp. She looked over her list. "Very good, class," she said. "And I'll run the maple sugar farm."

Abra put up her hand. "What about the laundry?"

"Pardon?" asked Miss Karp.

"Who's going to wash the miners' clothes?"

Smog piped up. "That's stupid. Miners didn't wash clothes. They liked dirt."

"Well, what about a store?" tried Abra. "Somebody has to run the store. And the post office. And the bank."

"Abra," said Miss Karp, "you do worry so."

"What's the point of having all those things?" asked Reuben. "It would be just like today."

"But a bank would be great," said Smog. "Then we could hold it up."

"Super!" Miss Karp made Reuben sheriff and banker.

The teacher leapt up and spun on one toe. "Be sure to bring your parents tomorrow," she said. "We're going to build a fort in the schoolyard, and we'll need all the help we can get."

Miss Karp sent everybody down the hall for music class. Everybody but Abra.

"I am very worried about your last test," said Miss Karp, holding up Abra's paper.

Smog made a face at Abra on his way out.

Abra stuck her tongue out at him.

"Abra!" scolded Miss Karp, looking shocked.

"Sorry," said Abra meekly.

Miss Karp waved the test. "Look at this. I asked you to write a few sentences about how pioneers got food. Other children wrote about planting grain and vegetables, making pickles, and salting pork. You wrote — "

"I know what I wrote," mumbled Abra. She had written that pioneers had brought their food over the mountains on mules.

"And I asked you to write about how pioneers' clothes were different from the clothes we wear today. You put down that pioneers wore lucky charms around their necks. And then you told me that bullrushes made delicious cookies!"

Miss Karp raised her eyebrows. "Well?"

Abra sneezed into her hanky. "I don't think that Granite Falls' pioneers lived like the settlers in your book," she explained. "Gold rush miners always wore lucky charms to help them find gold. And they didn't have time to plant anything because they spent all their time digging — "

"Oh, Abra!" sighed Miss Karp. "I can tell things are not going well at home, are they dear? You used to be such a good student."

Abra knew it. She was going to fail her best subject.

Miss Karp stood up.

"I will see your parents at the fort-raising," she said. She looked at Abra kindly. "We will have a heart-to-heart talk. I will solve all your problems," she promised. "Just see if I don't."

Abra had a feeling that all her problems were not going to be solved.

She had a feeling that they were just about to start.

Chapter 4

Timber-r-r-r

"This is so much better than my sister's class," said Kyra. "When they studied pioneer days, they only got to build log cabins out of pretzel sticks."

Abra and Kyra were standing in front of the school, helping Miss Karp hold up one side of the fort.

All the parents (except Abra's) were helping with the fort. Smog's mum, who was a boss at the lumber mill, had brought wood and a special kind of table saw. She wore goggles while she worked the saw. They made her look like some kind of wood-eating monster.

Reuben's dad was in charge of putting up the walls of the stockade. He wasn't too good at that, and the walls kept falling over. Every time they did, the principal, Mrs. Azzam, would run up and down the schoolyard in her high heels, shouting and pointing.

"Where are your folks?" asked Kyra.

Abra shrugged. "Floating around somewhere, I guess." In fact, she could see them sitting on the statue of Goldpan Annie that stood next to the town hall. Every time the fort fell over, they fell off the statue, laughing.

"My mum's the one with the camera," said Kyra proudly. "If she gets a good picture, it'll go in the *Gazette*."

"Yeah, well, my folks won't be in it," said Abra. "Pictures of them don't turn out too great."

Miss Karp glanced at Abra. "I don't see your parents yet."

Abra sneezed. Her eyes watered. She still had her cold. It didn't help any that Ma had rubbed garlic into her chest that morning.

Miss Karp clucked her tongue. "Don't worry, dear. I'll give them a call. I'm sure that — "

"TIM-BER-R-R!" Reuben's dad cried.

Abra and Kyra jumped out of the way. The wall crashed down right where they had been standing.

"Oh dear, oh dear," said Miss Karp, doing a head count.

Mrs. Azzam called the police for help.

Reuben's dad sat on the wall and put his head in his hands.

"Don't laugh!" Abra shouted at Ma and Pa. But they were already falling off Goldpan Annie's statue, kicking the air with glee.

Abra looked disgustedly at the mess of a fort. She watched as four police cars and two firetrucks screeched to a stop in front of her. Then she looked at Ma and Pa, who were still laughing so hard that they floated right out of their shoes.

Abra picked up her backpack. If she left everything up to her parents and Miss Karp, she was going to end up in a foster home. Which meant Smog's home. Because Smog's parents were the only foster parents in Granite Falls. And Smog was the meanest kid around, not to mention the stinkiest.

"Granite Falls didn't even have a fort!" she yelled at the firefighters as they rushed past her.

Then she headed home. To find a way to make her parents look good.

It was going to be a tough job.

Chapter 5

One More Chance

"I need new parents," Abra said to Goldpan Annie when she got home. Goldpan Annie lived with Abra's family.

"Doesn't everybody?" said Goldpan, flipping the pancake that she was cooking in her goldpan.

"Not like I do," muttered Abra. She told Goldpan about the school. And the fort that kept falling over and would never be ready for the fair. And about her parents, who just floated around, laughing.

"Miss Karp says she's going to call them," Abra fretted. "What am I supposed to do? Say, 'Sorry, they don't have a phone yet. Could you maybe send a telegram instead?'"

She could see it now. Miss Karp would march Abra home. She'd meet Pa and Ma. And Goldpan Annie. They'd feed her bear paws or coyote. Their hen would lay an egg in her purse. And when Pa and Ma went out front to wave goodbye, they'd disappear before Miss Karp's eyes!

"Ouch!" cried Goldpan Annie.

"That tooth again?" asked Abra. Goldpan Annie had bad teeth. That's because she was always breaking them by biting on the nuggets she found to see if they were real.

"Sure 'nuff," groaned Goldpan. "Would you mind?"

Granite Falls had no dentist in 1862. So Abra got out the twine. Tied one end to Goldpan's tooth. Tied the other end to the door latch. And slammed the door shut.

Out popped Goldpan's tooth.

"Thanks," said Goldpan. "That's much better."

Abra wondered what other kids' nannies were like.

Abra worked extra hard on her homework that night. She had to draw a picture of what Granite Falls' fort might have looked like. So she did.

Even though Granite Falls never had a fort.

Even though the whole idea was stupid.

Because the best thing to do was to lie low.

"Abra," Miss Karp declared the next Monday, "your parents are not in the phone book."

Abra looked down and noticed that one of her shoes was untied. She tied it up.

"Abra," said Miss Karp, "your parents did not come to the fort-raising. Or the school meeting."

"Yes, they did," replied Abra. "You just didn't see them."

Miss Karp shook her head sadly. "I've read about this kind of thing. There's no need to be so brave, child. I'm going to come home with you and have a little chat with them."

Abra choked on the gum she'd been chewing. Miss Karp whacked her on the back.

"You can't come," Abra spluttered. "They've got the flu. It's real bad. You wouldn't want to catch it. Honest."

Miss Karp sighed. She did four deep knee bends while she thought. Then she scratched her nose.

"All right," she said finally. "I'll give them one more chance. I'll see them at the Olden Days Fair — or else."

Abra didn't even want to think about what *or else* might mean.

Lying low and trying for good marks didn't seem to be working.

It was time for Plan B.

"Reuben," said Abra as they walked home from school, "I need your help."

"Yeah, right," laughed Reuben.

"Not with homework, silly," said Abra. Reuben's marks were only so-so. But he had a typewriter.

"I need you to type a note. From my pa."

Reuben stopped walking. He stared at Abra.

"You going to skip school?"

"Nope," said Abra. "My parents are."

"Give me a break," said Reuben.

Abra thought. She needed Reuben's help. Pa couldn't write at all. And the closest thing to a typewriter at the Kadabra house was a sharpened feather.

"Reuben," she asked, "can you keep a secret?"

"Sure," said Reuben.

"Say, Chew on nuggets and chomp on rock, if I break my promise, I'll eat my sock."

"What?"

"Say it!"

Reuben said it.

"Reuben," said Abra, "I think it's time you met my folks."

Chapter 6

Dear Ms Bruce,
we cannot visit you
this Friday, as I
have struck gold and
have to dig it up-
Egg

Plan B

At first Reuben wouldn't believe it.

"You're kidding," he said, standing in Abra's kitchen. "This is an act, right?"

Pa was sitting by the fire, toasting a rattler on a stick. Ma was weighing out some gold dust on a scale. Goldpan Annie was trimming her toenails with a pocketknife. And Bertha, the pig, was eating slops under the table.

"Pa," said Abra, "go outside."

Pa went outside.

As soon as his foot touched the front porch,

he disappeared.

"Horseshoes!" cried Reuben.

Pa stuck his foot through the doorway, into the house. It floated there, bodyless.

"Duckbills!" yelped Reuben.

Pa came all the way into the room, where Reuben could see him. Then he floated off the ground and brushed a cobweb off the ceiling.

"Beaver teeth! What are you?" gasped Reuben. "A magician?"

"Gold miner." Pa winked.

"Aw, Pa . . ." groaned Abra.

"Ghost," Pa said with a chuckle. "*And* a miner."

"Wow!" said Reuben. "What a great job. Can you walk through walls?"

"Only in the movies," said Abra. She sneezed.

Ma looked up from her scales. "That cold's getting worse, Abra," she said. "Better rub some goose grease on your chest."

"Later, Ma," promised Abra.

She turned to Reuben. "So, will you type a note for me? I want it to look good."

"Okay," agreed Reuben. He had brought his mum's typewriter in his backpack.

"Type this," instructed Abra. *"Dear Miss Karp. Mrs. Kadabra and I cannot visit you this Friday as we have a lot of work to do."*

"What kind of work?" asked Reuben. "She'll ask."

Pa set two tin mugs on the table. "Tell her I've struck gold," he said.

"No way!" protested Abra.

"Honesty's the best policy," declared Pa.

Abra scowled. "All right," she agreed. *"We cannot visit you this Friday as I have struck gold and have to dig it up."*

Reuben typed it.

"Now sign it, *Egerton Kadabra*."

Reuben couldn't spell Pa's name. He signed it, *Egg*.

Then he sipped his drink. "What's this?"

"Hot goat's milk."

"Not bad," said Reuben. "Could use some Strawberry Zip, though. Where's your bathroom?"

"Out back, next to the chicken coop," Goldpan Annie told him. "Don't forget to wash your hands at the pump."

Reuben looked at Abra.

"Are you sure you don't want to move in with Smog?" he asked. "They have a toilet in their house."

Goldpan Annie had finished trimming her nails. She slipped her feet into her big mining boots and clomped over to the table.

"That Miss Karp of yours is going to see right through that note," she said. "She's going to laugh the same way I laugh at fool's gold. And then she's going to round up that social worker and come straight over here."

Goldpan picked up Abra and Reuben's empty mugs.

"If'n I was you," she said, "I'd get to work on Plan C."

Chapter 7

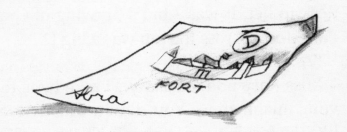

A Cry for Help

"Huh!" snorted Miss Karp. "Struck gold? I thought your father was an historian."

Miss Karp was reading Reuben's letter.

"He is," said Abra quickly. She crossed her fingers. "It's the way he talks. He struck gold in his . . . uh . . . research."

"Hmm," murmured Miss Karp. She got up from her desk and did some leg stretches.

Abra turned to go back to her seat.

"Wait!"

Abra waited.

Miss Karp pushed a piece of paper across the desk to her. It was Abra's drawing of Granite Falls' fort. Across the top was a big D.

"A *D*!"

Miss Karp nodded sadly. "I asked you to use your imagination. You didn't. This is exactly like the fort in your textbook. That's copying."

"But how could I use my imagination?" cried Abra. "Granite Falls never had a fort. I know that!"

"Nonsense," clucked Miss Karp.

Abra looked at her drawing.

Miss Karp sighed. She stopped doing leg stretches and sat on her chair instead.

"I know a cry for help when I hear one," Miss Karp said. She showed Abra her marking book. By Abra's name was a long row of A's. Then a row of D's. The row of D's wasn't as long as the A's. But it was getting to be.

"Don't worry, child. Everything will be all right soon." Miss Karp lowered her voice so the other kids wouldn't hear. "I'll talk to your parents at the Olden Days Fair. And if they don't come, I'll bring in Mrs. Clung."

Mrs. Clung! Mrs. Clung was Granite Falls' social worker. There wasn't much work for a social worker in Granite Falls. She was going to love the Kadabras!

Reuben couldn't believe it, when Abra told him later.

"My note didn't work?" he squawked. "But I typed it perfectly."

The class was in the schoolyard, getting ready for the fair. Reuben and Abra were painting the cardboard maple trees.

Reuben thought for a while. "Well, maybe your folks could do some hocus pocus. Turn Miss Karp into a cat, or something."

Abra gave him a look. "Yeah, right."

"Well, couldn't they at least make her lose her voice or her memory?"

"Ghosts," said Abra hotly, "do not do hocus pocus. Ghosts are just ordinary, everyday people. Only dead."

"Ordinary, everyday people," echoed

Reuben. "I get it."

"Reuben," said Abra desperately. "I've got a mother who rides to work on a mule. I've got a father who floats on the ceiling. And I've got a nanny who founded the town — more than a hundred years ago. I need help. Real help. Not jokes."

Reuben stopped grinning. He put on his wise face. "Abra, as Goldpan Annie said — it's time for Plan C."

Abra felt better already. "You're right, Reuben. It's time for Plan C."

She didn't know what Plan C was. Yet. But she knew what she had to do. She had to find a way to show Miss Karp that Abra was right about how Granite Falls' pioneers used to live. Then Miss Karp would change all Abra's D's to A's.

The paint was dry on the cardboard maple trees. They picked up two of them and carried them to Miss Karp's cardboard maple sugar farm.

"If you're thinking you're going to hang any

outlaws from those trees, think again!" hooted Smog. He was already wearing his black outlaw's kerchief around his face. It suited him.

Reuben made his fingers into a gun and pointed it at Smog. "Just you watch your step, outlaw! There's a jail waiting for you, you know!"

"Reuben!"

Reuben folded his gun into a fist and shoved it into his pocket. "Sorry," he said to Abra. "Where were we?"

"Plan C."

"So what is Plan C?"

Abra grinned. The shootout with Smog had given her an idea.

"Reuben," she said, "we are going to kidnap Miss Karp at the Olden Days Fair."

Reuben blinked. "We are?"

"Yes," said Abra. "We are. You and me. The Royal Engineers."

"I don't want to be a Royal Engineer. That sounds silly," said Reuben. "I want to be a sheriff."

"There weren't any sheriffs in Granite Falls," said Abra. "This was a British colony."

"Well, Miss Karp said — "

"That's just the point," said Abra. "Miss Karp is all mixed up. Maybe it's because she used to live in Hollywood. Somehow I've got to get her un-mixed."

"And kidnapping her will help?"

"Of course," said Abra. "Because if it doesn't — "

Just then, Smog stuck his finger in her back.

"Give me all your money," he growled. "Or I'll shoot."

If Plan C didn't work, Abra would be stuck with Smog. Twenty-four hours a day! She gave Reuben a meaningful look.

Reuben rolled his eyes.

"Okay," he said. "I'll help."

Chapter 8

Hand Over Your Prisoner!

Friday was Fair Day. All the kids were wearing their olden days clothes. Miss Karp was handing out maple sugar candy from her booth in the cardboard maple tree farm.

"Popcorn?" asked Reuben's dad. He was popping corn in a popper over a campfire. It was coming out all burnt.

"Er, no thanks," said Abra. She was already wearing her Royal Engineer's jacket. It was hot and scratchy. "Where's Reuben?"

"Doing sheriff stuff." Reuben's dad beamed proudly.

Just then Abra heard someone yelling. It was Miss Karp.

"Help! Sheriff! Help!" the teacher shrieked. Smog and his gang of outlaws had tied her up and were dragging her across the schoolyard.

Abra looked for the sheriff. He was tied up, too.

"Where's your deputy?" asked Abra, untying him.

"Who do you think tied me up?" retorted Reuben. "She joined the outlaws. Said they were more fun."

"Bang, bang!" shouted Smog, running by. "We've taken over the fort."

"Is this going to look bad on your report card?" asked Reuben's dad, coming over. "Do you want me to catch those bad guys for you?"

"No, Dad," said Reuben. "Thanks."

It didn't take long for Reuben to get into his red jacket and cap.

Then, standing in front of the fort, Abra

"Hear ye, hear ye!" she cried.

"Huh?" Smog looked over the top of the fort.

"We are here on behalf of Her Majesty, Queen Victoria!" shouted Abra.

"Are you nuts?" called Smog.

"We are the Royal Engineers! Hand over your prisoner!"

"Never!" shouted Smog. "Bang, bang! You're dead!"

Reuben fell to the ground, clutching his chest.

"Get up!" hissed Abra.

"Got the sheriff!" cheered the outlaws. "The sheriff is dead!"

Reuben jumped back up. "The sheriff is not dead!" he yelled.

"He's not a sheriff!" yelled Abra. "Granite Falls never had a sheriff. It had Royal Engineers. And I can prove it. Who wants to join the Royal Engineers?"

"Were they good guys or bad guys?" asked Smog.

"Good guys," said Abra. "Compared to you."

"Forget it!" yelled Smog.

"Well, can we have your prisoner?" pleaded Abra.

"No," said Smog. "I'll defend this fort to the death." He thought about it for a minute. Then he added, "Or until you bring me a year's supply of food for Pirate."

Abra looked at Reuben. "Pirate?"

"His marmorset monkey," said Reuben. "It eats crickets. Live ones."

Abra glared at Smog. "No way!" she yelled.

Plan C wasn't going too well.

It definitely needed Miss Karp. And Miss Karp was tied up.

"What would the Royal Engineers do?" asked Reuben.

Abra couldn't say. She knew they were supposed to catch outlaws, but she'd never actually seen them do anything but build roads.

"Well, then," said Reuben. "What will *we* do?"

Just then, Reuben's dad walked by. He was carrying a big pan of freshly made taffy. Reuben's dad made the best candy in town.

"Taffy pull!" yelled Reuben's dad.

"Hurray!" Everybody ran towards him. Parents. Kids. Teachers. Cowboys. Outlaws. And Smog, yelling, "Steal the taffy!"

Everybody but Reuben and Abra.

And the prisoner.

"Looks like your dad's solved our problem," Abra said.

They found Miss Karp in the jail.

"We don't have a key," said Reuben. "We're going to have to use force."

"Reuben," said Abra. "This jail used to be a cardboard box."

When they opened the lid, Miss Karp smiled. "Thank you for rescuing me."

Abra felt guilty. She knew Miss Karp hadn't planned on leaving the fair. Not with Smog on the loose. But . . .

"We're not rescuing you," she said. "We're, uh, escorting you to another fair."

Miss Karp looked a little confused. She picked up her purse.

"This Olden Days Fair isn't going the way I

thought it would," she said.

The two Royal Engineers and their prisoner walked out the front door of the fort. Past the candy. And out of the schoolyard. Without being seen.

Plan C was under way.

Chapter 9

The Worst Parents Ever!

"Wait here," said Abra. She left Reuben and Miss Karp on the porch and went inside.

"Ma! Pa!" she screeched. "Miss Karp is here!"

"You don't have to holler!" said Pa.

Abra looked around. Goldpan Annie and Pa were there. But —

"Where's Ma?"

"Bagging a cougar," said Pa.

"But," wailed Abra, "she promised to be here!"

"Hellooo?" Miss Karp yodelled, opening the door.

Reuben followed her in.

"You were supposed to wait outside," hissed Abra.

Reuben shrugged sheepishly. Then he wrinkled his nose. "What's that smell?"

"Bear fat," said Goldpan Annie. "Makes pretty good candles." She was stirring a bubbling vat over the fire.

Miss Karp's jaw dropped. She stared at Goldpan Annie. Goldpan Annie was a sight. Her hair was sticking out all over her head, because of the hot work she was doing. And she was wearing her good-luck bear claws around her neck.

"Miss Karp, I'd like you to meet my nanny, er, Ms Goldpan Annie," said Abra. "And this is Pa."

"How do you do," said Miss Karp, weakly.

Abra noticed Miss Karp didn't do a single spin. She really didn't seem herself.

"Tea?" offered Pa.

"Coffee, please," croaked the teacher. Abra saw her taking in the bear traps, the gold scales, the pickaxes, and Annie's new candles.

"Got some all ready," said Goldpan, plunking a mug onto the table. Miss Karp sat down on the chair Pa had built from crates.

"While I'm here, I'd like to talk about Abra —" began Miss Karp.

"Fine child," Pa beamed.

"Yes, er, well, she's been getting a lot of D's lately —"

"D's!" said Pa. "Isn't that wonderful!"

Miss Karp's eyes grew round as pancakes.

"I myself never went to school," said Pa, using a feather to dust Queen Victoria's portrait.

"Nor me either," said Goldpan.

"Never learned to read, myself," said Pa. "Told Abra she'd be better off panning for gold, but she insisted on going to school. Just like her Ma, that one."

Miss Karp took a big gulp of coffee. Her face was red.

"What Pa means," began Abra hastily, "is —"

She didn't need to finish, because Miss Karp was choking.

"What kind of coffee is this?" sputtered the teacher. Her eyes watered.

Abra looked at Goldpan.

Goldpan shrugged. "Dandelion root," she said. "Abra's Pa done ground it himself."

"Oh, great," Abra groaned.

"Why is your nanny making candles?" asked Miss Karp.

This was Abra's chance. Now she could explain her whole plan. How she had got Ma and Pa — well, Pa anyway — and Goldpan Annie to dress up as gold miners. How she'd decided that there could be two fairs on Fair Day, and that this one was her own Olden Days Fair. The way Granite Falls really was.

"She's doing it like a real pioneer," said Abra. "She knows how 'cause it's kind of a hobby —"

"Hobby my foot!" snorted Goldpan. "It's on account of my hobby that you can see to do your homework!"

Miss Karp looked at Abra. "Oh, I see," she

said. She scratched her nose.

"It's on account of my hobby that you can see your way to the outhouse at night," barked Goldpan.

"Oh, I see," said Miss Karp again.

"And if you don't get some squirrel stew on the fire, Abra Kadabra, you won't be having any dinner tonight," finished Goldpan, crossing her arms.

"Oh," said Miss Karp. "Squirrel stew. I see." She stood up.

"Abra, dear," she said, waving her skinny arms. "I can see why you brought me here. You poor, poor dear!"

"Wait a minute!" cried Abra. "You've got it all wrong!"

The back door flew open.

In came Ma.

"Give me a hand, will you?" Ma asked. She was pulling Bertha by a rope. The pig didn't want to come in.

Abra took Bertha's rope and gave it a yank.

The pig squealed and pulled the other way.

"What's wrong with her?" asked Abra. Usually, the pig ate at this time.

"She don't like the smell of cougar, I guess," said Ma.

She opened her sack. Out popped a big-eyed baby cougar.

"Supper?" gasped Miss Karp.

Ma fixed the teacher with a surprised stare. "Don't you know a pet when you see one? Why, I'd no more eat this cougar than I'd eat Bertha there."

"Ma, this is Miss Karp," Abra broke in desperately. She picked up the cougar. Plan C was not going well.

"Charmed," nodded Ma, scooping up a hen that had just walked in. "Always nice to meet someone with book learning."

"Mr. and Mrs. Kadabra," began Miss Karp. Her eyebrows were lifted so high they disappeared under her hair.

"Clem," said Ma.

"Egg," said Pa.

Reuben grinned at Abra. "This is lots more

fun than when she came to see *my* folks," he said.

"I have to tell you, Clem and, uh, Egg, that I intend to do something about this right now." Miss Karp snatched up her bag. "I'm going to get Mrs. Clung."

"Lovely," said Ma. "Why, we haven't had visitors in years."

"Years and years and years," agreed Pa.

Miss Karp looked shocked.

She also looked angry.

"Why, you two are the *worst* parents I've ever met! And *this* is the worst place any child in Granite Falls has ever had to live in!

"Something must be done about this *today*!"

Chapter 10

Welcome to 1862

"Wait!" yelled Abra.

Everybody looked at her.

"Abra," said Reuben, "I don't think Plan C is working."

"That is because I haven't explained Plan C yet," pointed out Abra. "Everybody knows Plan C always works. Whoever heard of Plan D?"

Abra turned to Miss Karp.

"Welcome to the Abra Kadabra Olden Days

Fair," she announced.

"Pardon?" said Miss Karp, and sneezed.

"Tsk, tsk," said Ma. "You should rub on some goose grease for that cold."

"I don't have a cold," scowled Miss Karp. "I have an allergy. To cats."

"No cats here," said Goldpan Annie, who was feeding the cougar from a baby bottle.

"Ah-CHOO!"

"Abra," murmured Reuben. "Plan C?"

"Welcome to my Olden Days Fair," Abra began again, loudly. Everybody looked at her.

She pointed around the room.

"Everything you see here is exactly the way it was in 1862," she declared. "Everything is just like the days of the Cariboo Gold Rush."

"Exactly," said Reuben.

Miss Karp looked pointedly at Bertha the pig. "I hardly think — "

"Miners had pets, too," said Abra. "They just didn't get into the history books."

Miss Karp raised her eyebrows. "How do you know?"

Abra coughed. "Well, my parents . . . "

"Were there," put in Pa.

"Are experts on the subject," said Abra, nudging Pa with her elbow.

"Indeed we are," agreed Pa.

Miss Karp sniffed. "Your parents are behind this. That explains everything."

"Oh, no," said Abra. "This whole thing is my idea."

"Totally," said Reuben. "She made me do it."

Miss Karp stared at Abra. "Why did you do this?"

"I wanted to show you what Granite Falls really used to be like," said Abra. "So you'd change some of my D's back into A's. And I wanted you to meet my parents. So you'd see how nice they are. But I guess things didn't go so well." She sighed.

Miss Karp wasn't saying anything. She was just staring at the Kadabras. And the cougar.

"I guess not," said Miss Karp at last.

Then she smiled.

She didn't say why she was smiling.

She just smiled.

"I think I'll stay to lunch after all," she said.

"Squirrel stew?" offered Ma.

"Why not?" replied Miss Karp.

"Bread?" asked Goldpan Annie. "Fresh from my goldpan?"

"Lovely," said Miss Karp.

"Rattler on a stick?" asked Pa.

Miss Karp looked at Abra.

Abra shrugged. "It's barbequed," she said.

Miss Karp sneezed. "Well, maybe just a little," she said weakly.

"While we're cooking," said Goldpan Annie, "would'jer mind helping with the chores?"

Miss Karp giggled. "Why, certainly. Chores were certainly part of every pioneer's life. What's to do?"

Goldpan Annie pointed to a pile of jackets and pants that went almost to the ceiling.

"Those have to be washed. By hand."

"Goldpan!" screeched Abra.

Goldpan shook her finger at Abra. "They have to be done. It's washday."

Abra explained to Miss Karp. "Forty-five Royal Engineers dropped by this morning. They're in the neighbourhood, keeping the peace."

"Hah-hah," said Miss Karp. "You've certainly gone to a lot of trouble to make your point."

"Granite Falls never had a sheriff," said Reuben sadly.

"Granite Falls never had too many bad guys, either," declared Abra. "The Royal Engineers are building a road. That's why their clothes are so dirty. They pay two gold nuggets for washing them."

"Gold nuggets!" Miss Karp smiled. "Isn't that sweet?"

"Here's your bucket," said Goldpan Annie, dropping a bucket next to the teacher. "Here's your soap."

"Best soap in the Cariboo," claimed Ma. "Made it myself."

"Hah-hah!" said Miss Karp.

Abra brought the water from outside. "We don't have a tap," she explained.

"Of course not," said Miss Karp. And chuckled.

It took Miss Karp and Abra and Reuben a long time to wash the Royal Engineers' jackets.

"Only two nuggets for all this work?" complained Reuben.

They were hungry by lunch time.

"Delicious," said Miss Karp, after one forkful of stew. "What is it?"

"Squirrel stew," Pa told her. "My own recipe."

"Hah-hah," said Miss Karp. "And where are the rattlers?"

"Burned 'em," said Pa sadly.

Miss Karp smiled more widely. "What a shame. But the bread is delicious. You say you made it in a goldpan, Annie?"

"Yep," boasted Annie. "Nothing to it. A little flour. A little water. A pinch of salt. Then you spit on it to make it rise — "

Miss Karp laughed so hard she fell off her chair.

Abra helped her up.

"So," Abra said, "now do you believe me that the pioneers of Granite Falls didn't plant pumpkins or make maple syrup — "

"Critters!" exclaimed Goldpan Annie. "Ain't no time for that. What with finding gold, and doing laundry — "

"Chasing claim jumpers. And catching cougars," said Ma.

"Picking dandelions," added Pa. "For coffee."

"And do you believe that there were no sheriffs?" asked Abra hopefully.

Reuben looked at his hands. They had blisters. "After washing forty-five big red jackets, even I believe in the Royal Engineers."

Miss Karp did four knee bends.

That was a good sign.

She did a leg stretch, two side kicks, and a spin.

That was a very good sign.

Then she looked at Abra.

"No."

Chapter 11

Goose Grease and Garlic

"No?" cried Abra.

"No!" shouted Ma and Pa, Goldpan Annie and Reuben.

"No," said Miss Karp. "I don't believe that pioneers ate squirrel stew and rattlers-on-a-stick and goldpan bread."

"Huh!" said Goldpan Annie, sniffing.

"What about the Royal Engineers?" asked Reuben.

"Well, maybe there were Royal Engineers,"

Miss Karp acknowledged. "I'll have to check in my book."

"Oh," said Abra sadly. "I guess I'll fail history, then. And I guess you'll bring Mrs. Clung. And I guess I'll have to live at Smog's house."

"Well," began Miss Karp. But she couldn't say any more because she began to sneeze. And sneeze. And sneeze.

"Goose grease and garlic?" offered Ma.

"Ah-CHOO!"

"I think that means yes," said Pa.

"Does it, Miss Karp?" asked Abra.

"Ah-CHOO!"

"I don't think so," said Reuben.

"Nonsense," scoffed Ma. "She's sneezing. Of course she wants goose grease."

Ma handed the teacher the jar of goose grease. "Try it," she ordered. And Miss Karp did.

Right away, she stopped sneezing.

Her eyes stopped watering.

Her nose stopped running.

She sat back down on her chair, looking surprised.

"Just think of that!" she said.

Ma beamed.

"Bertha!" shouted Abra. "Stop that!"

Bertha had her nose in Miss Karp's bag. She was chewing on something.

Miss Karp's history book.

"Oh, Bertha!" moaned Abra. "You've ruined everything!"

"That's Miss Karp's favourite book," said Reuben.

Abra and Reuben looked at Miss Karp.

Abra put her hands out.

"What are you doing?" asked the teacher.

"Handcuff me," cried Abra. "Take me to Smog's house. I'm ready."

Miss Karp chuckled. Then she laughed. Then everybody laughed.

"Why are we laughing?" asked Reuben.

"Because," said Miss Karp, "I'm not taking Abra anywhere."

"You're not?" asked Abra, surprised.

"No," said Miss Karp. "I may not agree with your view of history — "

"Huh!" snorted Goldpan Annie.

"Though I must say you have put a lot of thought and," she pointed to Bertha "and energy into this. You deserve an A just for that."

"And if she gets an A, she gets to stay?" asked Reuben.

Miss Karp looked at Pa and Ma. "I wasn't really worried about Abra's marks," she told them. "I was worried about the reason for them. I thought . . . well . . . "

Abra spoke up. "You thought I had crummy parents."

"Ahem." Miss Karp cleared her throat. "In a way, yes. Your parents didn't come to any meetings. They didn't care about your schoolwork. I thought they didn't love you."

"Imagine!" said Ma.

Miss Karp picked up the jar of goose grease and garlic. She rubbed a little more on her throat.

"Mr. and Mrs. Kadabra," she said, "I have never met a more, uh, unusual set of parents than you."

"Uh-oh," groaned Abra.

"But it is very clear that you love Abra. You turned your whole house inside out to help with her history project — "

"Not really . . . " said Pa.

"And you invented the most wonderful cold medicine for her," said Miss Karp.

"Yes," said Ma.

"It's okay to have unusual parents," declared Miss Karp.

"It would be a lot easier to have ordinary parents," mumbled Abra.

Miss Karp jumped out of her chair and twirled.

"In other words, Abra should stay right here," she announced.

"Yay!" hollered Reuben.

"Hurray!" cried Abra.

"Yahoo!" shouted Ma and Pa and Goldpan Annie.

Miss Karp shook hands with Ma and Pa.

"I hope you'll come to next year's Olden Days Fair," she said.

"Certainly," said Ma.

"I'll see you there, then," declared Miss Karp.

"Well . . . " Pa grinned mischievously.

"The thing is, they're awfully busy . . . being historians," warned Abra.

"Oh," said Miss Karp.

The cougar jumped into her arms, and she patted it.

Then she smiled.

"Well," she said, "if ever I need a second opinion about the history of Granite Falls, I'll know where to come."

"Here," said Abra.

"The coffee's always on," said Pa.

Recipe for Prospector's Bread

For rising bread: make a thick paste of flour and water, and add anything you desire for flavor. This must be made to ferment, so add yeast. If you have none, add a portion of ripe raw fruit, or spit on the mixture. Set aside in a warm place until it foams to twice its size. Add enough flour to make it stiff. Knead it until dry. Let it rise until it cracks. Knead it again, and form into loaves. Let it rise, and cook it in an oven.

From *Cariboo, the Newly Discovered Gold Fields of British Columbia, Fully Described by a Newly Returned Digger*, Darton and Hodge, 1862.

About the Author

Maureen Bayless keeps a goldpan handy just to try out Goldpan Annie's recipes. Her three sons think she makes the best "spit-raised" pan bread since the Cariboo gold rush.

Maureen and her family live in Vancouver, where she is working on several other books. Her first book for Scholastic was *Howard's House is Haunted.*